BREAKOUTS

THE
WITCH'S
DAUGHTER

Jill Atkin

Ransom

ONE

Normally, when my big brother Josh comes home from work, he wanders in and slumps down in the kitchen with a can of coke. This time it was different. He was red in the face as if he'd run a marathon, and he was gasping for breath.

'What's up?' I asked.

'It's the Town Hall,' he panted. 'It's on fire. There's chaos in town. They've closed the High Street.'

I sprang from my chair and dashed to the window. We can't see the centre of town from our house, but even though it wasn't quite dark, there was a strange orange glow over the houses opposite.

'I can see it!' I shouted. 'Wow! It must be some fire!'

'It is … and the whole town is there gawping at it.'

I felt a shudder shoot right through me. The Town Hall was iconic. I've always loved its intricately carved stonework, the market place underneath its arches and its central clock tower. Standing in the middle of the High Street for hundreds of years, it was part of our town and part of everybody who has ever lived here. I had to go and see the fire for myself.

'I'm going down there,' I said, as I pulled on my jacket.

'It's chucking out heat like an erupting volcano. Don't get too close.'

'Josh!' I pulled a face. Just because he's five years older

than me and I'm a girl, he doesn't need to treat me like I'm only four, instead of nearly fourteen.

'Well, I know what you're like: downright nosy!'

He's got me in one. I stuck out my tongue as I checked my phone was in my pocket and ran outside.

The glow grew brighter as I raced down the road and I began to dread what I was going to see. But I still wasn't prepared for it. When I came round the corner into the High Street, I stopped dead and stared. Red and yellow flames licked like dragon's breath from every window; billowing clouds of black smoke mushroomed high above the old Town Hall; water jets arched from firefighters' hoses into the flames, but they were fighting a losing battle. The fire had completely gutted the building. I felt gutted, too, and incredibly sad. I know Josh thinks I'm a bit of a dare devil, but I like the security of familiar things, too, and I suppose this old building was part of that. As I watched, an icy shiver slid up my spine, even though I could feel my face and the front of my body roasting in the heat.

'Hi, Jess!'

I turned round. It was my friend Lewis, who lives in the flats at the far end of my street. I like Lewis. I've known him since we were kids. As he pushed through the crowd, I noticed his face was lit up with excitement and his eyes glowed, like mirrors reflecting the fire.

'Brilliant, isn't it?' he said.

'Yes,' I said, but not in the way he meant it. The fire was brilliant all right, but it was also devastating.

'Have you taken any photos?' he asked.

'Not yet,' I said. To tell the truth, photos didn't seem important at that moment, but I pulled out my phone and took a few photos of the fire. We peered at them on the screen. Then we stood for ages, totally spellbound by the flames. Eventually, we dragged ourselves away.

There was no sign of Josh when we both got back to my house, but I was pleased to find that Gran

Braithwaite was home. She's great, my Gran! She understands me a lot better than Mum does. It's cool having her to 'keep an eye on us' while our parents are away on holiday. But this evening, she was sitting at the kitchen table, resting her chin on her hands.

'Hello, Lewis,' she said.

'Hi.'

I felt kind of sick as I went and stood beside Gran. She put her arm round me and peered up into my face.

'You OK?' she asked.

I shook my head.

'I'm feeling rather delicate, too,' she said. 'The Town Hall's always been very special to me.'

'Me, too.' I gave her a hug. 'We've been down there. I've taken some photos.'

'I'd like to see them,' Gran said.

I held out my phone, but she shook her head. 'No good showing me that,' she said. 'It's too small. With my eyesight … can't you make them bigger?'

'I'll print them out,' I said, heading for the stairs. 'I won't be long.'

Lewis and I went upstairs to my room. My hands shook slightly as I turned on the printer and waited for it to warm up.

'Why am I feeling like an icicle's stuck inside my T-shirt?' I asked.

'Don't ask me,' said Lewis. 'It's only a burning building.' But he was fidgeting. I could tell it was getting to him, too.

The printer began to whirr away, but now I felt so itchy I began pacing about the room.

At last, the first photo slid out. It was spectacular with flickering flames leaping into the night sky. The second photo was even more dramatic. It showed the firefighters and the arc of water jets silhouetted against the burning building. We studied the first two photos while the third one printed.

'They're great,' said Lewis.

I didn't answer. I was staring at the final photo. I gripped the table, fighting the waves of nausea that came over me.

'What's up?' asked Lewis. 'You look as if you've seen a ghost!' He leant forward and peered at it. 'Wow!' he whispered.

It was slightly blurred, and yet I could tell what I was staring at. There, standing on the narrow flat roof at the front of the building, surrounded by flames that darted like flickering tongues at her long white dress, was a woman!

TWO

'Oh my god,' I whispered. 'That's hideous.' My head spun. I had to sit down on my bed and take some deep breaths. Lewis sat down beside me.

'She must have burned to death,' I said.

'Yeah.' He spoke like an automaton. 'I reckon.'

'I wonder who she was.' We sat in silence for a while, staring at the photo.

'Have you printed those photos out yet?' Gran called upstairs. I snapped out of my trance.

'Yes!'

But I couldn't move. Screwing up my eyes, I tried to persuade myself that it was just a smudge on my camera lens, but it was no use. It was definitely a woman standing there.

'What was she doing up on the roof?' Lewis asked.

I shrugged. I didn't have an answer. I heard footsteps on the stairs, then Gran hurried into the room. I held out the photo. 'Look at this,' I said.

Gran took the photo and gasped. 'Oh my! Poor woman,' she said. 'What a way to die! But surely someone must have seen her up there in the flames.'

'They can't have done,' said Lewis. 'Or the firefighters would have rescued her.'

'I suppose so,' said Gran. She had another long look at the photo. 'We'd better take this to the police. Oh, dear. This has been a terrible day for me.'

Gran drove to the police station and we showed the photo to an officer behind the desk.

'It certainly *looks* like a woman,' he said, peering through his glasses. 'But the building has been searched thoroughly. No one was found. It must be a shadow or a mark on the lens.'

'It *can't* be,' I said. 'It's a woman. I know it is. Look!'

The officer frowned at me. 'OK, young lady,' he said. 'You obviously know best. We'll get the fire brigade to investigate, just to make sure. I'll hang onto this photo.'

'OK,' I said, but I didn't like his tone, really patronising, and I wasn't sure whether to believe him. He didn't sound very enthusiastic. I opened my mouth to say something I might have regretted, but Gran took my arm and steered me out of the door. She got in the car.

'I'll see you later,' I said. 'I'm going back to the High Street. I want to have another look.'

'All right,' said Gran.

'Coming, Lewis?' I asked.

'You bet.'

A thick fog hung over the whole area and there was a strong acrid smell of smoke in the air. The Town Hall was burnt to a blackened shell, like a haunted house in a horror movie. The roof was almost completely demolished with a few beams like a skeleton's ribs remaining. I just stared. Why did I feel so upset over a stupid old building? We stood for ages, watching the fire fighters who were still damping it down. I felt another icy snake slither up my spine.

'Let's take a copy of the photo round to the *Mercury* office tomorrow,' Lewis said, as we eventually tore ourselves away. 'It's a fantastic story. They'll love it.'

'Great idea,' I said.

Josh was stretched out in front of the TV in lounge lizard mode when I got home.

'I keep getting this strange feeling,' I said. 'Like ice-cold reptiles slithering up and down my back.'

'I bet you've got a cold coming, little sis,' he said. 'Why don't you ask Gran to mix you one of her potions?'

I smiled. Gran Braithwaite's herbal medicines were famous for miles around! I'd been dosed up against a cold many times before and I knew exactly what she'd give me. Tincture of Echinacea in water with ginger and garlic!

'I don't need her medicine,' I said. 'I don't think it's a cold.'

Josh frowned. 'What d'you mean?'

'It's different – ghostly – something that started as soon as I heard about the fire.'

'Rubbish!' Josh turned back to the TV.

Next morning, I called for Lewis and we hurried to the local newspaper office. The man on the front desk wasn't interested in our story at first, but when we refused to leave and then insisted on showing the photo to the Editor, we were suddenly treated like celebrities. We had to answer thousands of questions.

'This has the makings of a fabulous story!' said the Editor. 'We're just in time to run it on the front page tomorrow.'

THREE

The rest of the day dragged. Josh was at work and Lewis had to rush off to meet his dad in town. Gran had gone back to her house for the day, so I was on my own.

I couldn't settle to anything, despite all the usual possibilities like swimming, shopping or seeing my friends. I didn't feel like doing any of them. I had no energy for swimming and no money for shopping. As for seeing friends, somehow this seemed so special I didn't want to share it with them. I had an inkling that my obsession with a photograph might make them think

I'd lost it. Anyway, most of them were away on holiday.

The icy sensation was still there, but now it was more like dozens of freezing fingers racing up and down. I wrapped myself in my coat and scarf, but I couldn't get warm. I kept being drawn to the photo. Although it was slightly blurred, I sensed the woman's strange mood. Her dark eyes seemed to be staring right at me. Her long blonde hair was blowing wildly in the strong wind and her white robe was flapping like a flag. She looked quite young. Who was she? Curiosity was burning my brain.

After lunch, I left the house and hurried to the High Street. Crowds still hung about outside the high fencing that had been erected. I stood by the 'NO ENTRY' sign posted on the fence and stared. There were no flames, no smoke, just the blackened shell of what had once been a beautiful building. I bit my lip, fighting back tears. Was I upset about the building or the woman? I didn't know.

I hadn't heard whether the fire brigade had searched the ruins again. But if they had looked and found no one, where had she disappeared to? Suddenly I gasped as a creepy thought slipped into my head: supposing she was a ghost!

I didn't think I'd sleep, but I must have done and when my alarm woke me up early next morning, I got ready as quickly as I could, left a note for my sleeping Gran and went round for Lewis.

The Editor had kept her promise. As soon as Lewis and I dashed towards the newsagent's I spotted the A-board outside.

The Mercury
TOWN HALL FIRE LATEST
Local kids' discovery

We rushed inside. The headline on the front of the newspapers piled on the counter jumped out at me immediately:

WHO IS THE MYSTERY WOMAN?
Does anyone recognise her?

Underneath the headline, there was a close-up of *the* photograph. I leaned over the counter and began reading.

'Hey!' said Mr Patel.

I know Mr Patel quite well as I'm always in his shop, but I stepped back guiltily and looked up at him, to discover he was grinning.

'D'you like the photo?' I asked. 'I took it!'

'I might have known it was you,' he said. 'It's great! Fantastic!'

I grinned back.

'So, my famous friends,' he said, 'you're not leaving until you've told me the whole story.'

When we finally managed to escape from Mr Patel's shop with several copies of the paper, we headed for the park. We sat on the swings and read the report on the fire and all the details of our interview. The fire brigade had carried out another meticulous search, but they hadn't found a single bone of a body in the ruins of the Town Hall. So far, no one had reported a missing person. So who was she and how did she end up out on the roof?

'I think it's really weird,' Lewis said. 'It's like she just vanished into thin air!'

'You know what?' I said. 'You might think I'm mad saying this, but it suddenly struck me yesterday when I was in town. I think I may have actually taken a picture of a ghost!'

Lewis laughed. 'Ghost? Whose ghost?'

'That's what I aim to find out,' I said. 'Are you in?'

Lewis's eyes began to shine. 'Yeah!' he said. 'Where do we start?'

We went to his place and spent hours surfing the net. We found some great information on ghosts, old buildings, local history and suspicious deaths. But there was nothing connected to the old Town Hall. All this time, I could not get rid of the sensation of those freezing fingers zipping up and down my back. I had goose pimples all over my arms. There was something uncanny going on. It was getting to me.

That evening, I was still feeling very strange. 'I'm not hungry,' I said to Josh when he came in from work. 'I keep feeling shivery.'

'I told you you've caught a cold,' said Josh.

'Not that kind of shiver,' I said. 'It's like a ghost … '

Josh frowned. 'You're talking a load of rubbish,' he said. 'That photo must be a trick of the light. Forget it.'

'But … ' There was no point in saying any more. But there was no way I could *forget* it! I decided I needed to talk to Gran. She was sitting in the lounge.

'I don't feel well,' I began, 'but I don't need medicine.'

'I know.'

I stared at her. 'It's to do with the woman in the burning building,' I said.

Gran nodded.

'Gran,' I began, wondering if I dare ask. 'Do you believe in ghosts?'

'Of course I do,' she said.

'Do you think the woman in the photo could be a ghost?'

'I do! You know what I think? A long time ago, something terrible must have happened to that young woman on the roof.'

My heart began to race. 'D'you really believe that?' I said.

'Of course.'

I hugged her. 'That's great. I'm so relieved we think alike!'

We studied the photo. I felt my throat tighten and my face burn, yet my spine felt as if it was being jabbed by a hundred sharp icicles.

'But who was she? And how long ago did she live?'

'From the style of her dress,' said Gran, 'I guess she lived well over a hundred years ago. I've no idea who she was, but I believe … ' She paused and put her hand on my arm.

'What?'

' … your shivers may be her ghost trying to communicate with you.'

FOUR

I couldn't believe what Gran had just said. A ghost trying to communicate with *me*? For a few seconds I couldn't speak. My brain swirled like a whirlpool.

'Why me?' I blurted out at last.

'*You* took the photo, didn't you?' said Gran. 'But I can't help feeling it's more than that.'

'Do you mean I'm *haunted*?'

Gran smiled. 'Not haunted!' she said. 'I don't know enough about it to explain, but I'll ask some of my contacts. They're more into that kind of thing than I am.'

I was so excited that Gran believed in the ghost, and I really hoped one of her contacts would know what to do about it. The thought of there being a ghost was mind-blowing, but I didn't quite fancy walking round with it forever.

'Will it do me any harm?' I asked.

'I shouldn't think so,' she said. 'So don't go worrying about it, but I'd keep what I've said to yourself if I were you.'

I nodded. 'Not even tell Lewis?'

'Well, yes, tell Lewis, of course, but no one else,' she said. 'We don't want all kinds of cranks trying to get in on the act! Let's keep it a secret between the three of us, at least until I've found out more.'

Lewis punched the air when I told him. 'Yes!' he said. 'I *knew* there was something spooky about all this!'

The next few days dragged by so slowly that I became tense and bad-tempered. One afternoon, Lewis and I were still searching the internet at his place. We'd reached another dead end.

'I'm sick of staring at this screen,' I snapped. 'Let's leave it for now.'

'No, we can't give up. We might have missed something.'

'We've looked on every site and found nothing.'

'Well, *I'm* not chickening out.'

'Chickening out! You … ' I only just stopped myself saying something I might regret. I took several deep breaths. 'I need to go out.'

We hung around the shops, then the park, but I

couldn't relax. My back felt like an icy breeze was blowing across it. It was as if the ghost was impatient, too.

'I wonder what your Gran's doing,' Lewis said, sitting motionless on a swing. 'Have you asked her lately?'

'Of course I have, but she's keeping everything to herself. It's almost a week since the fire. I'm beginning to wonder if she'll ever come up with anything. And Mum and Dad will be back soon.'

We walked slowly to my house and opened the back door. Gran was sitting at the kitchen table, drinking tea. I rushed in and sat down opposite her.

'Any news?' I asked. 'I've been dying to hear what your contacts think!'

'Yeah! Me, too,' said Lewis.

'These things take time,' Gran said. 'Calm down and I'll tell you what I've found out. Have a cup of tea.'

She thrust a cup into my shaking hands and poured one for Lewis. I gulped mine back in one go then put the cup down and waited.

'Most people I spoke to had seen your photo in the papers,' she said. 'But they were all as puzzled as I was. Then, only yesterday, I found someone who might be able to help us.'

FIVE

I gripped the table as a massive shiver shot through me like a lightning strike.

'That's great news!' I said as the shiver faded. 'Who?'

'An old lady – and I mean *very* old. I think she's over a hundred. Her name's Mrs Lister.'

'Where does she live?' I was on the edge of my seat, ready for action.

'In a tiny cottage on the outskirts of town,' said Gran.

'Have you been to see her?'

'Yes. I've met her. She claims to have special powers. Since she was a young woman she says she's had contact with people "on the other side", as she puts it.'

'You mean dead people? Stiffs?' Lewis's eyes were wide. 'I like it!'

My pulse was thumping. I could feel it in my head. I had an uncanny feeling that the old woman was going to solve the mystery. I really hoped so. 'And she can still do this, even though she's so old?' I asked.

Gran nodded. 'She's very weak and pretty deaf, but she keeps regular contact.'

'Creepy!' said Lewis.

'So what did she say about our photo?' I didn't want

to waste a second now. I needed Gran to get to the point.

'She keeps pretty much to herself, so she hadn't heard about the Town Hall fire. Nor does she read the *Mercury* so she hadn't seen the photo until I showed her.'

I felt disappointed. I don't know why I was expecting her to be onto our case immediately. 'Will she be able to help?'

'Well,' said Gran. 'I hope so. I don't know whether there is any connection, but it appears she's been pestered for a while by someone in distress.'

'What kind of distress?' Lewis asked.

'A voice, she told me, calling a name she couldn't quite decipher. She seemed relieved when I found my way to her house and told her about you and the photograph. We had quite a long chat. She thinks there might be a link!'

'Really?' More shivers took over my whole body. I desperately hoped the old lady was right. There *had* to be a connection. 'So will she see us?'

'Yes,' said Gran. 'She was very enthusiastic. Her cheeks became quite rosy as we talked. I hope it won't be too much for such an elderly person.'

I leapt up. 'Come on then, what are we waiting for?'

'Hold on!' said Gran, who hadn't moved a centimetre. 'Not today. Tomorrow, Saturday. Four o'clock. After her afternoon nap.'

I slumped back in the chair. 'I can't wait that long!' I said.

'Well, you'll have to. She won't see you before then.'

'Can I come?' Lewis asked.

'Of course. I told her about you, too. She'd like to meet both of you.'

34

I didn't sleep very well that night. I felt so twitchy and the shivers just would not go away. I kept texting Lewis. His replies showed he was as restless as me.

I still felt the same next morning. I couldn't eat any breakfast or lunch. By early afternoon, I was raring to go. Josh looked from me to Gran and back again.

'You're both insane,' he said. 'Why can't you drop the whole thing?'

'You've got no imagination,' Gran answered with a sigh. 'Not like Jess and me.' She turned to me. 'All set?'

'Yeah.'

While Josh and Gran argued about ghosts and whether it was ridiculous or not thinking anyone could communicate with the dead, I sent a text to Lewis, telling him to come over.

Then, while I waited, I wandered from room to room, unable to keep still, while fighting off the shivers and trying to calm myself down. I was certain this was going to be an amazing experience I would never forget.

'What kept you?' I asked Lewis when he arrived.

I didn't wait for his answer, but dashed past him into the street. He raced after me, but we soon had to slow down to Gran's pace. We hadn't a clue where we were going. After a ten-minute bus ride, Gran took us along streets I had never been to before. We must have been walking for about twenty minutes when she stopped at a broken down old gate.

'This is it,' Gran said quietly as she opened the gate. There was a slight tremor in her voice and I realised she must be feeling as nervous as I was.

SIX

We hammered on the door several times and waited a lifetime before the door slowly creaked open. Mrs Lister was tiny. Not even up to my shoulder. Dressed in a black dress that reached to the floor, with two dirty pink slippers poking out beneath, she was the tiniest, most wrinkly old lady I had ever seen. Her nose was hooked like the beak of a hooded crow and her eyes and mouth were like deep crevices amongst the wrinkles of her face, which was pale beneath her knot of white hair. She stood there, squinting against the sunlight.

'Hello, Mrs Lister,' Gran shouted. 'I've brought my granddaughter and her friend to see you. You remember, we talked about them yesterday.'

Mrs Lister frowned and for a moment I was afraid she had forgotten all about Gran. Then her face cracked in a smile and she beckoned us in with fingers like the sharpest talons. We followed her shuffling footsteps in pitch blackness along a passage and into a small square room. The curtains were closed and the room was almost as dark as the passage, but it was lit by two oil lamps. I could make out a table in the middle with four chairs round it.

'This is creepy,' Lewis whispered in my ear. I nodded, aware that he was standing very close to me. I guess he was feeling apprehensive, too.

'This is Jessica.' Gran's shout echoed across the dark room.

'Jessica?' said Mrs Lister in her quaky little voice. 'Oh yes, I remember now.'

She seemed very vague. A sinking feeling developed in my stomach. Were we making a big mistake coming here? Was Josh right after all? Was this all a load of ridiculous nonsense? Mrs Lister wasn't really going to help us at all.

Then she put her head on one side like a bird and her eyes began to shine. She looked straight at me.

'Your Gran has told me everything I need to know,' she said. 'Sit down.'

She took the seat facing the door and pointed to the other chairs. Gran, Lewis and I obeyed, with me opposite Mrs Lister, Gran on my left and Lewis on my right. Mrs Lister immediately closed her eyes. We sat there in silence for so long I thought she must have gone to sleep, but I couldn't take my eyes off her. At last, she began to sway backwards and forwards, first humming, then chanting and talking in a weird language. Her face began to twitch as her mouth opened and closed in a strange torrent of words.

The atmosphere was charged with electricity. I had goose bumps all over as I sat stone still with the others, watching, waiting and listening.

Suddenly, I felt sure there was some other being in the room. Was it another person? Or a ghost? I was convinced that whoever or whatever it was had come to stand behind me and was breathing icy breath down my neck. I dare not turn round, but continued staring at Mrs Lister without moving a muscle.

Then I sensed the something touching my shoulder. I whipped round, but there was nobody. Just our dark shadows silhouetted on the walls.

At that moment, Mrs Lister shrieked. The harsh sound cut right through my brain and my stomach clenched in a vice-like grip.

'Jessica!' Mrs Lister wailed with her eyes still tightly closed. 'I have a message for Jessica.'

SEVEN

I froze in my chair, terrified. What did this outburst mean? I dare not glance at Gran or Lewis, but I felt their eyes on me. I'm sure I must have turned a deathly pale.

'I'm Jessica,' I heard myself say. 'What's the message?'

'Someone wants to speak to you,' croaked the little old lady. 'I'm getting it loud and clear. Someone with a story to tell. Listen, Jessica, listen. Someone needs your help.'

I sat forward in my chair and leaned my elbows on the table. 'Who?'

She was silent for a few minutes. Then she opened her mouth again.

'Someone is telling me a tale. I have been asked to pass it on to you.'

'I'm listening,' I whispered.

'Many, many years ago ... ' Mrs Lister began, 'there lived a woman who was skilled in the practice of herbal medicine.'

I gasped. 'That's a coincidence!' I whispered. 'So is my Gran!'

'Shh!' hissed Gran.

'*My name is Mary.*'

Gran's name!

Mrs Lister's voice had abruptly become stronger and less shrill, as if it wasn't her speaking. Was this the voice of her contact? I had no time to worry about that as the voice continued. *'I was famous for miles around and everyone called on me if they were sick. I mixed medicines from my vast store of herbs.'*

'That's what Gran does.'

'Shh!' Gran said again.

'I was also a midwife, delivering babies at all times of night or day.'

I didn't speak this time although I knew Gran had been a midwife, too, when she was younger. The parallels were uncanny.

'Sometimes things didn't go exactly as they should,' said the voice. *'And one dark stormy night, whilst travelling along a country lane on my way to a delivery, I bumped into a man. My hair was loose and bedraggled as I had been buffeted by the wind and my clothing flapped in an*

alarming way. I must have looked a fearsome sight because I terrified the man. He rushed to the nearest house and accused me of hag-riding.'

'What's hag-riding?' asked Lewis, who had been staring silently at Mrs Lister all this time.

'It was a form of witchcraft,' whispered Gran, 'when a person came and terrified others by night … Let Mrs Lister go on.'

'The man created such pandemonium that everyone came out of their houses. He pointed an accusing finger at me and called me a witch. I had to flee. I knew what they used to do to witches in the olden days and I didn't want that to happen to me.'

I had visions of someone being burned at the stake or drowned in a ducking stool!

The voice paused and Mrs Lister slumped lower into her chair. It looked as if this was exhausting her.

'*By that time, I had been blessed with a son and a daughter. They were happy, healthy children aged ten and eight. They were being cared for by a neighbour while I was out travelling, but when news of the accusation of witchcraft reached her ears she threw my children out. She wanted nothing further to do with them or with me.*'

There was another pause. I sat holding my breath, trying not to interrupt again. But I was desperately curious now. What was she going to reveal?

'*This malicious neighbour contacted the authorities and told them I was a witch. I have no idea what happened to my children from that moment on.*'

I wanted to ask how Mrs Lister could possibly be doing this and was she speaking the truth, but I bit my lip. I didn't want to stop her now.

'*For years, I travelled far and wide across the country, searching for my missing children, but I never found them. Finally, I gave up the search, presuming they had come to an early grave. I died of a broken heart.*'

45

I felt tears welling in my eyes. I hadn't realised how emotionally involved I was becoming in the sad story. I found it difficult to believe that the life of someone I had never heard of before today could affect me in this way. I heard Lewis sniff beside me and I glanced at Gran. Her lips were set in a grim line and her eyes were full of sadness.

Then, without warning, a breath as cold as death blew down my back and my teeth began to chatter uncontrollably.

EIGHT

Mrs Lister folded her arms, rested her chin on her chest and closed her eyes.

'You can't stop now,' I cried. 'We've only heard half the story.' I desperately needed to know more about the connection between Mary, whose voice we had heard, and the woman in the photo, whose ghost was strengthening its grip on me.

'What's going on?' Lewis whispered. Gran shrugged.

'Mrs Lister.' Lewis tapped the table loudly in front of her.

The old lady lifted her head as her eyes snapped open. She looked around at the three of us. 'Oh, sorry, did I nod off?' she said. 'Where was I?'

'Mary died of a broken heart,' I said.

'Oh, I remember now. I lost touch with Mary the instant she said she died.'

'Is there any way you can find out what happened to her children?'

'I hope so. Let's try again. I shall need your help this time.'

'What do you want us to do?' asked Gran.

'Close your eyes, lay your hands on the table and concentrate. Maybe someone else will make contact.'

I shut my eyes. We waited and waited, but nothing happened except for the icy grip getting stronger. I was tempted to open my eyes, but forbade myself. I didn't want to jeopardise our chances.

At last, Mrs Lister gasped, then groaned. 'I'm getting a new voice,' she croaked. 'It's not as clear as Mary, but I believe it is calling for Jessica ... Yes, I'm certain now.'

'*Is there anybody here named Jessica?*' This voice was much higher. She sounded younger.

'Yes, that's me.' I opened my eyes. Mrs Lister was rocking back and forth again as the new voice continued.

'*I am twenty summers old, the daughter of Mary, who was wrongly accused of being a witch. Our neighbour, who was caring for us while Mother was away, threw my brother and me out of her house. A few days later, men came and found us hiding out in a barn. I do not know what happened to my brother, but I was dragged kicking and screaming to the Town Hall ...*'

'The same Town Hall?' Lewis gasped.

'Shh!'

' … *where I was questioned about Mother. Fearing for her life, I refused to answer their questions and after many days, the men gave up and sent me to a distant orphanage.*'

The voice gave a stifled sob. '*I spent many long years in the orphanage, but I have never forgotten my mother and brother. I have been wandering ever since, searching for them. At last, I am come back to the Town Hall where they questioned me all those years ago.*'

'It's the woman on the roof speaking!' I whispered. 'I'm sure of it.'

'*Oh, Sirs, help me, please, help me!*' she cried. There was a short pause.

'*Why won't you help? You must know what happened to my mother. Tell me!*' Another pause.

'No! I will not leave!' she screamed. 'I will stay here until you help me!'

Mrs Lister rocked more violently. Her face was contorted with agony and her bony talons were clenched tightly in her lap. She took a deep shuddering breath before the voice began again. 'Jessica, hear my tale …'

My body was rigid, frozen, as if I'd been dunked in the Arctic Ocean. She was talking to me! 'I'm listening,' I said again.

'These cruel men will not help me. Of course, they are lying. I believe they have hidden my mother and brother away. I will search the building from top to bottom. I am determined to find them. Now I'm opening doors, running along corridors, climbing stairs.' She was panting and I began to feel breathless, too.

'Here is another set of stairs. Up and up, I climb. I find a door. It is bolted. Ah, I can release the bolt. The door opens onto the roof!'

'Creepy!' whispered Lewis.

'Shh!' hissed Gran.

'Don't go out there!' I screamed, but then I heard her footsteps, birdsong, men shouting. Her voice spoke more quickly.

'If I move nearer the edge I can see the world down below: the bustle of everyday life. It is unimportant to me. My only wish is to find my family.'

'Be careful!' I shouted. I was frantic, yet I knew it was hopeless. How could I stop something that had happened so long ago?

'It is windy and raining, but what do I care?'

I was panting as if I'd just won the 100 metres.

'The slates are slippery. The wind is gusting. I am so weak and thin. I have no strength against such a wind … ahhhhhhhh!'

Mrs Lister's toothless mouth widened and an ear-shattering scream filled the room. I dug my fingernails into the palms of my hands, not daring to speak or take my eyes off her. Then she slumped back in her chair, exhausted.

Silence. My body shook as I tried to fight off an attack by millions of jagged shards of ice. So many questions bombarded my brain. Was this it? Was I going to be left in the depths of permafrost? Why had she asked for Jessica? Why me? Was it just because of the photo? Or was there something else really spooky that she hadn't said yet?

'*I fell to my death.*' I could hardly hear the voice. I waited for her to continue, but there was only silence.

'What was the message?' I whispered at last. 'How can I help you?'

The old woman gave a shuddering sigh and pulled herself up in her chair. '*I still want to find my mother and brother.*'

I leant forward to hear her.

'*I want you to find them for me!*'

'Why me?'

'*Because my brother was called Joshua. And my name is Jessica.*'

My head reeled and ice demons held me in a vice-like grip. But nothing could have prepared me for what she would say next.

'*Our surname was Braithwaite. And my brother, Joshua, was your great, great, great grandfather!*'

NINE

I must have passed out. The next thing I knew, I was lying on a sofa at the side of the room and Gran was leaning over me. Lewis hadn't moved. Mrs Lister sat slumped with her head on the table.

'What's happening?' I asked. I sat up and promptly lay down again as waves of dizziness mingled with Arctic ice took me over. Talking to the ghost hadn't got rid of my shivers! 'Mrs Lister can't stop there. We need to know more if we're going to solve this.'

'It's all right,' said Gran. 'Before she nodded off she told me there is one last part of the message. Let's see if we can wake her ... gently!'

Ten minutes later, we were ready to leave. I'd written everything down. Through Mrs Lister, Jessica had given us a full list of instructions.

I don't remember leaving the house. As we hurried along in silence, I felt weak-kneed, just as when I'd recovered from the flu. I gripped Gran's arm and wrapped my coat tightly around me, but I tried to concentrate on what we had to do. I was glad Lewis and Gran were with me, especially because of where we were heading!

'It's a good job you don't live in the olden days,' I managed to say to Gran, when we were well away from Mrs Lister's house. 'You might have been called a witch! It could have happened to you!'

'I know,' she said.

We reached the churchyard gate and stopped. The place looked eerie as the early evening sun cast long dark shadows across the gravestones.

I gulped and fought back the urge to run away.

'Here goes,' whispered Gran. 'Where's the yew tree?'

It was uncanny. There it stood in the far left hand corner of the churchyard, exactly as Jessica had described it. When we stood under its wide-spreading branches a few minutes later, I wondered how much it had grown over the years since Jessica's death. Gran read her scribbled notes.

'Face west,' she said.

'That's into the setting sun,' said Lewis.

We counted seven graves from the left, then three rows down. It took us right to the boundary of the churchyard.

'This must be Jessica's grave,' I whispered, feeling a cold hand pulling me towards a long, uneven mound of grass. There was no headstone. No name ... an unmarked grave.

I stood for a moment, not knowing what to do now we had found Jessica's grave.

'Let's see if we can find the others,' whispered Gran. 'Before it gets dark.'

It took us quite a while to find the second grave, with a simple headstone naming,

Mary Braithwaite
1835-1879
aged 44 years

'If only Jessica had known how close her mother was,' I whispered as we stood looking down at the second grave.

The last light from the setting sun cast a deep orange

glow around the churchyard as we searched for the third grave. At last we stood in front of a much bigger, more ornate gravestone:

Joshua Braithwaite
1860-1940
aged 80 years

'My great, great, great grandfather,' I said.

Gran nodded. Then I saw her shiver.

'Let's go,' she said. 'We'll come back tomorrow and do what we have to do.'

TEN

We never did tell Josh about what happened. We thought he'd just repeat what he'd said before – that it was a load of rubbish. Nor did we tell Mum and Dad, although they asked rather a lot of demanding questions when they got back. Gran and I agreed that we would keep it as our special secret.

Several weeks later, the grass had been cut around the unmarked grave, a priest had performed a short service beside the grave and a simple headstone had been laid at one end, engraved,

Jessica Braithwaite
1863-1883
aged 20 years
R.I.P

Gran, Lewis and I stood by the graveside.

'Rest in peace,' we said as we laid flowers. Then, as I took a last look at the grave, I felt warm for the first time in weeks.

Suddenly, a thought flashed into my brain. I started to run. Lewis was right behind me as I raced home. I leapt up the stairs several at a time and flung open my bedroom door. The photo was on my bedside unit and I snatched it up. By the time Lewis ran panting into the room, I was staring at it. I held it out to him.

'Look!'

The Town Hall was burning fiercely. Jets of water arched high into the flames. But the ghost of Jessica Braithwaite, the witch's daughter, had gone!

I thought it was all over, but Gran stopped coming round to our house and she didn't answer her phone. Worried that she might be ill, I called round on my way home from school.

There was no answer when I knocked, so I went round the back. Gran was perched on a stool at the kitchen table. I banged on the window. She looked up and stared at me for a moment as if she didn't recognise me. Then she blinked several times, slid from her stool and came to let me in.

'Our visit to Mrs Lister brought back strange memories for me,' she said.

'Yeah?'

'When I was about your age, I was haunted, too.'

I gasped. 'Not by Mary Braithwaite?'

'Yes, though I never knew who it was until now. Her voice in my head led me to take up herbal medicine, and that's never left me. That's why I searched so hard to find Mrs Lister for you. I didn't want *you* to be haunted for ever.'

'And her voice in your head? Is it still there?'

'No, it's gone – like your shivers.'

I hugged Gran.

'They're both at peace now,' I said.

Jill Atkins began her working life as a Primary school teacher, but eventually escaped and ran a Bed & Breakfast for several years. This is when she began writing in earnest. She's had over 60 books published with a variety of publishers.

Jill lives with her husband in West Sussex and loves spending time with her children and five grandchildren.